Pebble Plus

Penguins!

# King Penguins

by Jody S. Rake

PEBBLE
a capstone imprint

Pebble Plus is published by Pebble
1710 Roe Crest Drive, North Mankato, Minnesota 56003
www.mycapstone.com



Library of Congress Cataloging-in-Publication Data
Names: Rake, Jody Sullivan, author.
Title: King penguins / by Jody S. Rake.
Description: North Mankato, Minnesota : Capstone, an imprint of Pebble,
[2020] | Series: Pebble plus. Penguins! | Audience: Age 5-6. | Audience: K to Grade 3.
Identifiers: LCCN 2019008833 |
ISBN 9781977109378 (hardcover)
ISBN 9781977109439 (ebook PDF)
Subjects: LCSH: King penguin--Juvenile literature.
Classification: LCC QL696.S473 R357 2020 | DDC 598.47--dc23
LC record available at https://lccn.loc.gov/2019008833

**Editorial Credits**
Donald Lemke, editor; Ted Williams, designer; Kelly Garvin, media researcher;
Katy LaVigne, production specialist

**Photo Credits**
Minden Pictures/Goetz Eichhom, 21; Shutterstock: Alexey Seafarer, 11, Amplion, 4, Anton_Ivannov, 1, Designua, 4, Janelle Lugge, cover, jo Crebbin, 19, kwest, 7, Ondrej Prosicky, 5, Rich Lindie, 17, Roger Clark ARPS, 13, 15, Vyshnivskyy, 9

Design elements: Shutterstock/Rashad Ashur

Printed and bound in China.
1654

# TABLE OF CONTENTS

# THE KING OF PENGUINS

The king penguin is the second biggest penguin. It stands about 37 inches (94 centimeters) tall. It weighs 30 to 35 pounds (13 to 16 kilograms).

60 inches
(152 centimeters) tall.

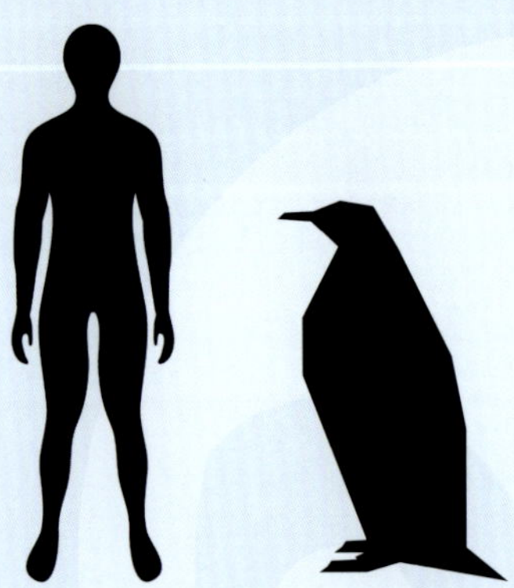

37 inches
(94 centimeters) tall.

King penguins are colorful birds. Their feathers are silvery-black, white, and orange. They also have an orange stripe on their black beaks.

# THE LOUD CROWD

King penguins live on islands around Antarctica. They live away from ice and snow. King penguins live in large, noisy colonies. They often call to one another.

Penguins are birds that don’t fly. King penguins use their strong flippers to swim and hunt. They catch lanternfish and other prey with their beaks.

Chicks grow warm, fuzzy down. They look like teddy bears with beaks. In a few months, they grow waterproof feathers.

The parents continue to feed the chicks, but not every day. The parents leave their chicks and go hunting. The chicks stand in a group to keep warm.

# A KING'S LIFE

King penguins are grown up at about five years old. Killer whales, leopard seals, and other predators hunt king penguins. King penguins may live 20 to 25 years.

# GLOSSARY

**beak**—the hard, front part of the mouth of birds

**colony**—a large group of the same kind of animal living together

**down**—the soft, fluffy feathers of a baby bird

**feather**—one of the light, fluffy parts that cover a bird's body

**flipper**—one of the long, flat upper limbs of a penguin; flippers help penguins swim

**hatch**—to break out of an egg

**predator**—an animal that hunts other animals for food

**prey**—an animal that is hunted by another animal for food

**waterproof**—not allowing water to soak through

# READ MORE

**Hall, Margaret.** *Penguins and Their Chicks: a 4D Book.* Animal Offspring. North Mankato, Minn.: Capstone Press, 2018.

**Schuh, Mari.** *Penguins.* Black and White Animals. North Mankato, Minn.: Capstone Press, 2017.

**Terp, Gail.** *Penguins.* Wild Animal Kingdom. Mankato, Minn.: Black Rabbit Books, 2017.

# INTERNET SITES

*Kiddle: King Penguin Facts*
https://kids.kiddle.co/King_penguin

*PenguinWorld*
http://www.penguinworld.com/types/king.html

*KidZone: Penguins*
https://www.kidzone.ws/animals/penguins/

# CRITICAL THINKING QUESTIONS

1. What do king penguins look like?
2. How do king penguins catch their prey?
3. How do king penguin parents take care of their eggs?

# INDEX